D1626808

WITHDRAWN FROM
THE LIBRARY
UNIVERSITY OF
WINCHESTER

KA 0063630 4

British Library Cataloguing in Publication Data
Bonnici, Peter
Amber's other grandparents.
I. Title   II. Kopper, Lisa
823'.914[J]   PZ7
ISBN 0–370–30671–6

Text copyright © Peter Bonnici 1985
Illustrations copyright © Lisa Kopper 1985
Printed in Great Britain for
The Bodley Head Ltd
30 Bedford Square, London WC1B 3RP
by Cambus Litho, East Kilbride
First published 1985

KING ALFRED'S COLLEGE
WINCHESTER
SCHOOL RESOURCES CENTRE
YF/BON   X22968

Amber's Other Grandparents

PETER BONNICI

Illustrated by Lisa Kopper

THE BODLEY HEAD
LONDON

At breakfast I knew that something was going on.
No one else finished their cornflakes.

Then Mummy put on her green sari
instead of her clothes for going to work.

She stuck a red dot on her forehead and put some black stuff on my eyes.

I thought perhaps we were going to a party.

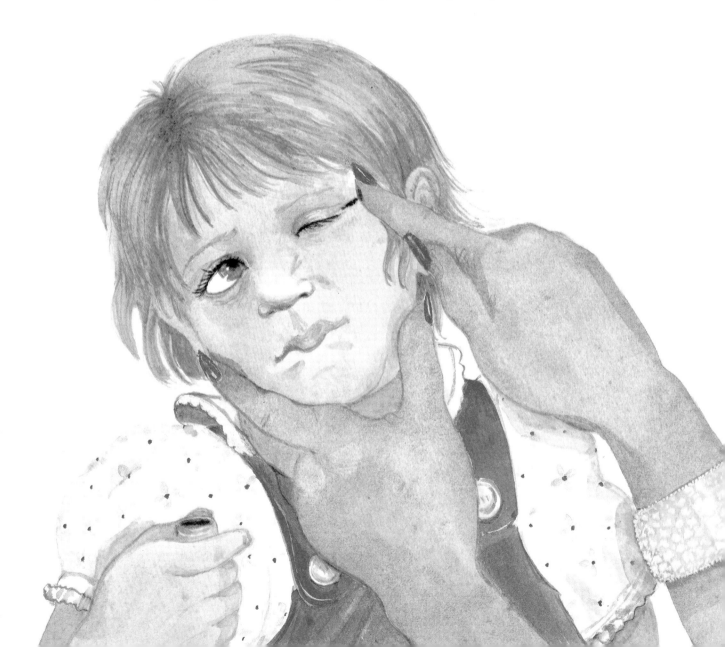

When Daddy saw us all dressed up, he called Mummy a Rani. He poked my nose and said, "That means queen where your mother comes from."

In the car Mummy told us that we were going to see our grandpa and grandma. And I said, "We don't usually dress up for that."

Mummy laughed. "These are your *other* grandparents – from India."

"Are we going to take a plane to meet them?" I asked her.
"Don't be silly," Timothy said. "They're coming here
to stay with us for a holiday."

Mummy spotted them first and began to wave.
I thought they looked very nice.
But Timothy said, "*They're* not our grandparents."

Our real grandparents were very different.

My new grandma didn't know how to speak English.
But Mummy seemed to understand what she said.

My new grandpa did speak English – but in a funny way. "Come on, little Amber," he said to me. "Tiger got your tongue, or what?"

At lunchtime grandpa said, "Let us take food in the Indian manner."

That was fun. We all sat on the floor and ate with our fingers. Daddy showed me how to do it.

After lunch my new grandma gave me a mango.

Then she looked up at Mummy and looked back at me and quietly said, "Prejent."

Everyone laughed and clapped and Mummy said, "*Jee ha, present!*"

I think I'm going to like my other grandparents, after all.

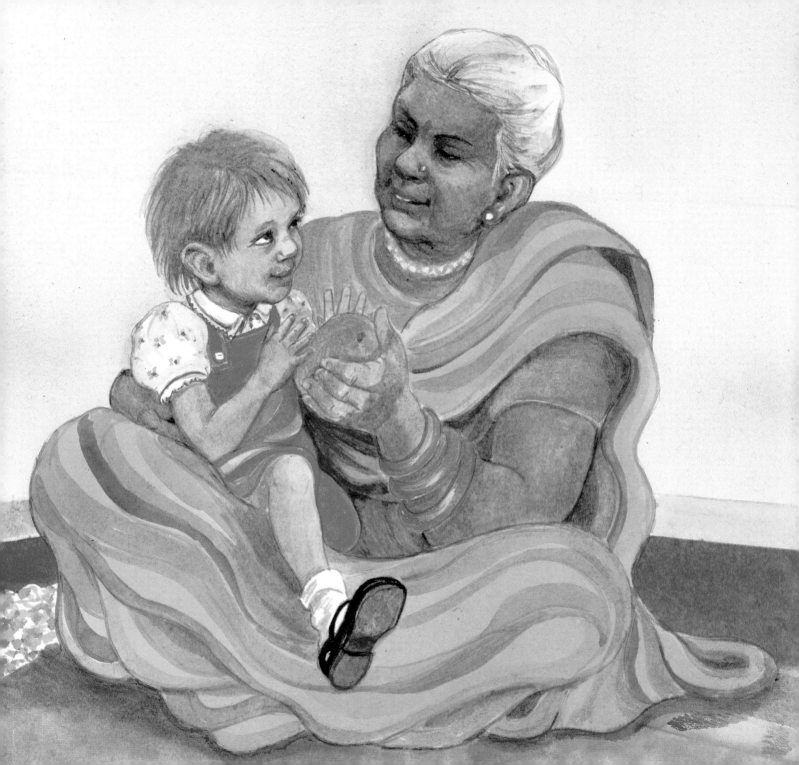